This very lovely book belongs
to me and my name is:

....

....

This book belongs to

_____

#ilovereading2020 #wearemaumee

Illustrated by Jacqueline East
Written by Rachel Elliot

First published by Parragon in 2009

Parragon
Queen Street House
4 Queen Street
Bath BA1 1HE, UK

ISBN 978-1-4075-4470-0

Manufactured in China

Please retain this information for future reference.

Princess

Mia and the Big Smile

Bath New York Singapore Hong Kong Cologne Delhi Melbourne

Running a Kingdom is a serious business.

The Butler took it very seriously.
The Queen took it very seriously.
The King took it very seriously indeed.
Everyone in the Kingdom took it very seriously.

Everyone except Princess Mia.

Princess Mia just couldn't be serious.

Every day, Princess Mia sat at the royal breakfast table and ate ruby-red tomatoes with fried eggs and toast. She could not help but

tap her feet.

And when she put on her royal boots and went into the yard, she could not help but

turn cartwheels

around the royal flower borders.

It was all extremely tiresome.

There wasn't a moment's peace in the castle. The King's courtiers kept taking long vacations. The Queen was very bad tempered, and meals were never on time because Cook was so distracted.

One day, Princess Mia danced through the palace kitchen with her ribbon twirler, and Cook forgot all about the King's afternoon tea and cookies.

"You must be more serious!" the King told his daughter.

"I can't help it," said Princess Mia.
"Everything is so much fun!"

"What do you mean?"
asked the King.

"I wake up in a soft, silken bed," explained the Princess.
"Who could help but bounce up and down and dance around?"
"Hmm," said the King.

"At breakfast I have fried eggs with toast,
and tomatoes as red as rubies," said Princess Mia.
"Who could help but tap their feet?"

"I see," said the King. "What else?"

"I have the palace gardens for my playground," said Princess Mia.

"Who could help but turn cartwheels?"

The King looked extra-specially thoughtful.

Next day, Princess Mia
woke up on a camp bed,
under a scratchy blanket.
"That's odd," she said.
"I'm sure I went to sleep
in a four-poster bed."

Then a big smile spread
across her face and she
bounced out of bed.

"What fun!" she said.
"I'll pretend that I am
an ordinary little girl!"

When the princess danced
in to breakfast, the King was
so surprised that he dropped
a piece of toast on his royal
dressing gown, butter side down.

The Butler placed a very small bowl of cereal in front of the princess. Princess Mia stared at the bowl of cereal. The King stared sadly at the buttery stain on his dressing gown.

Everyone else stared at Princess Mia's big smile.

"Ordinary little girls eat cereal for breakfast," Princess Mia told herself. She tapped her feet as if she could hear music, and started to eat her cereal.

Her big smile stayed exactly where it was.

After breakfast, the Princess was sent to the schoolroom.
"No playing in the yard today," said the King.
"Good," smiled Princess Mia. "I am being an ordinary little girl, and going to school is very ordinary!"

Princess Mia did schoolwork all day long. But her tutor could not stop her from humming. Once, when she was humming a very catchy tune, he forgot himself and joined in.

After school, the Princess looked at the King.
She looked at his serious face.
She looked at his down-turned mouth.

She put her arms around him and gave him a kiss.
"You need to smile more, Daddy," she said.

Princess Mia showed the King how to dance around the palace gardens and do cartwheels. The King wasn't very good at them but he kept trying again and again.

Suddenly, his face wasn't quite so serious.

Princess Mia showed the King how to make a kite SWOOP through the sky like a bird.

The King got his string tangled once or twice, but he did quite well for a beginner. His face was looking less serious by the minute.

Princess Mia led the King back into the throne room.
She gathered everyone in the palace together and played the
biggest game of hide-and-seek that anyone had ever seen.
The King caught the Butler, who wasn't very good at hiding.
"Well done, Daddy!" cried Princess Mia.

The King's mouth *twitched.*

It started to *turn up* at the corners.

Then he gave a beautifully *big smile!*

"I had forgotten about dancing and cartwheels!" he said with glee. "I thought that they were a waste of time!"

"Silly Daddy," said Princess Mia.
"I had forgotten about kite flying," chortled the King.
"I had forgotten all about hide-and-seek!"

The King danced around the throne room with the Queen, and on his face was the biggest smile in the whole Kingdom! He did a cartwheel and bounced onto his throne to pass some laws.

"From now on," said the King, "I decree that everyone MUST do at least ten cartwheels a day! We will teach silliness in schools! And everyone in the palace will have one hour off a day to practice kite flying and bouncing!"

The King gave Princess Mia
a beautiful charm necklace.
"This will remind you that
everyone needs a little bit
of silliness to keep them
smiling," he said.

"Silly Daddy," said Princess Mia. "I've always known that!"
And she danced out of the palace to play.